frog

This book belongs to

. . . .

 bat

 armadillo

 unicorn

yak

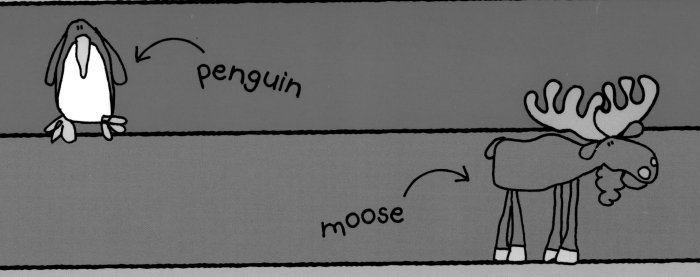

penguin

moose

Zebra's rainbow

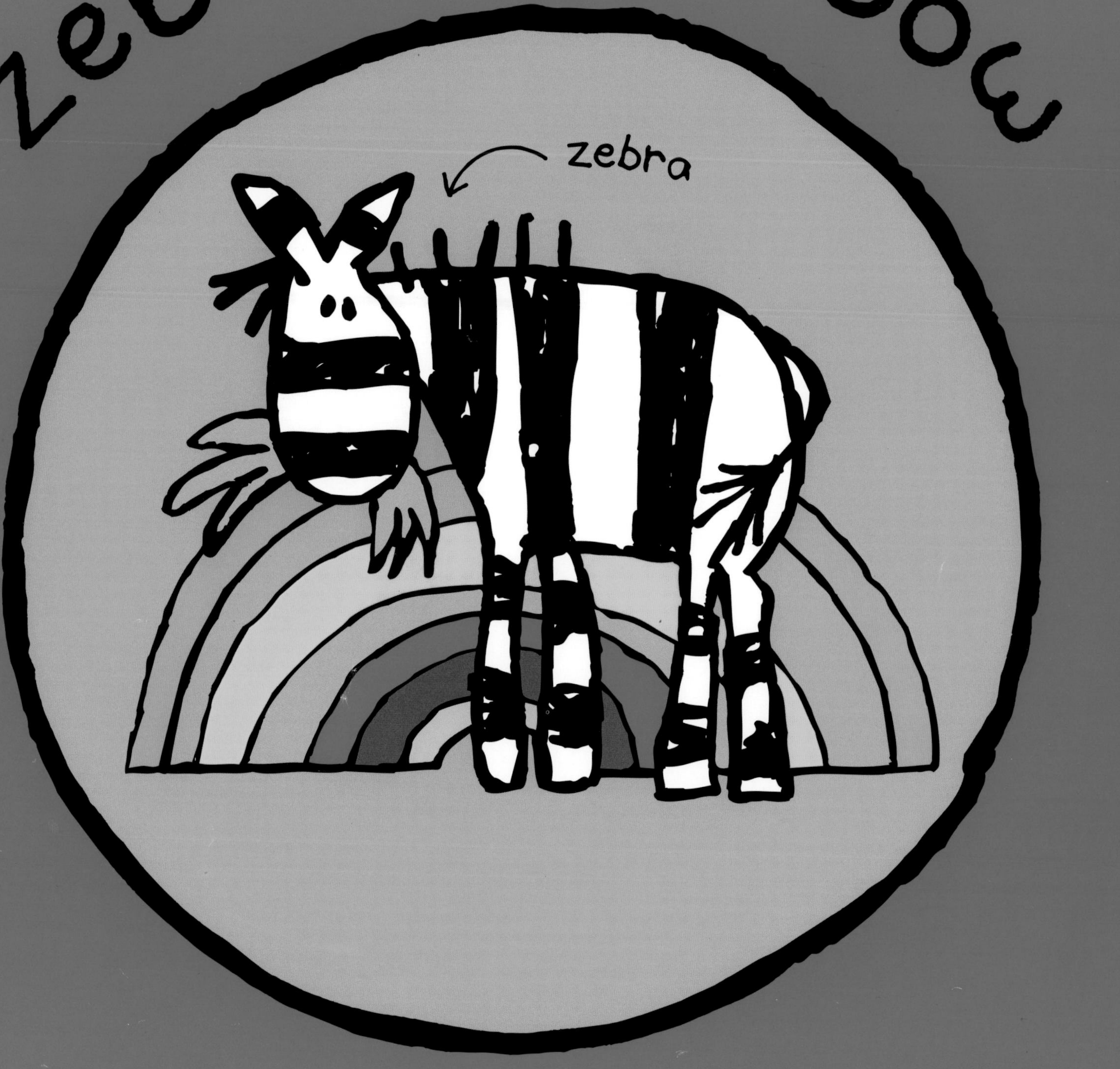

Zebra
is having
a party.

I wonder what my friends will bring?
excited zebra
I love parties
stripy

Bat brings
a wobbly
red jelly.

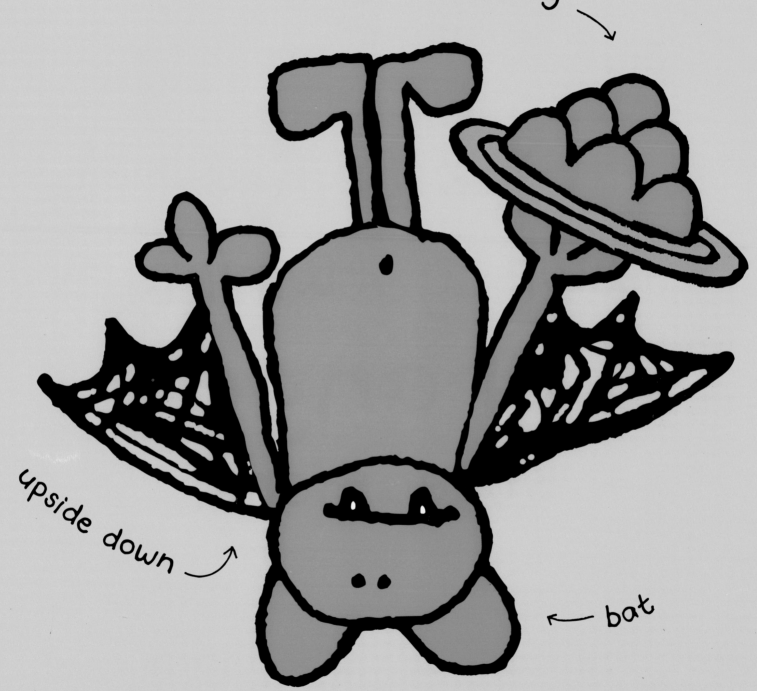

wobbly wobbly jelly

upside down →

← bat

Yak brings twisty, twirling **orange** streamers.

Lion brings **yellow** balloons.

Armadillo brings games wrapped in **green** paper.

Penguin brings **blue** party hats for everyone.

Moose brings **purple** juice drinks.

Unicorn brings **pink** cup cakes.

a rainbow party!

Can you match each object to the right colour in the rainbow?

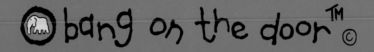

OXFORD
UNIVERSITY PRESS

Great Clarendon Street, Oxford OX2 6DP

Oxford   New York

Auckland Bangkok Buenos Aires Cape Town Chennai Dar es Salaam
Delhi Hong Kong Istanbul Karachi Kolkata Kuala Lumpur Madrid Melbourne
Mexico City Mumbai Nairobi São Paulo Shanghai Taipei Tokyo Toronto

Oxford is a registered trade mark of Oxford University Press
in the UK and in certain other countries

Text © Oxford University Press 2003

www.bangonthedoor.com

The moral rights of the author and artists have been asserted

Database right Oxford University Press (maker)

First published 2003

British Library Cataloguing in Publication Data available

ISBN 0-19-272565-3 (paperback)

3 5 7 9 10 8 6 4

Typeset in Freeflow

Printed in China